This edition published by Parragon Books Ltd in 2014

Parragon Books Ltd
Chartist House
15–17 Trim Street
Bath BA1 1HA, UK
www.parragon.com

ISBN 978-1-4723-7981-8

Printed in China

Disney · PIXAR
MONSTERS
UNIVERSITY

Bath · New York · Cologne · Melbourne · Delhi
Hong Kong · Shenzhen · Singapore · Amsterdam

When Mike Wazowski was six years old, he went on a field trip to Monsters, Inc. He snuck inside a child's bedroom and saw a Scarer at work. That one amazing moment made Mike realize he wanted to be a Scarer himself when he grew up!

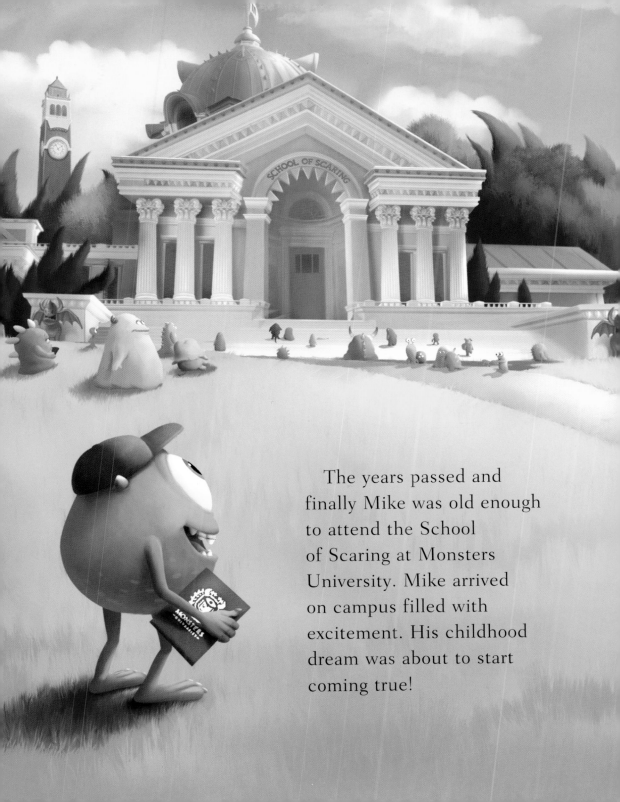

The years passed and finally Mike was old enough to attend the School of Scaring at Monsters University. Mike arrived on campus filled with excitement. His childhood dream was about to start coming true!

One of Mike's classmates was a huge monster named Sulley. He belonged to the Roar Omega Roar fraternity. Sulley and the RORs made fun of Mike. They thought he was too small and funny looking to be a Scarer.

Mike was determined to study hard and ace his final exam. Meanwhile, all Sulley did was mess around. He thought that being big and having a loud roar were enough to make him the best Scarer.

During the final exam, Mike and Sulley got into a roaring face-off. They accidentally broke Dean Hardscrabble's prized scream can. Hardscrabble continued giving Mike and Sulley their exam. Then she decided that neither of them would be staying in the Scaring Programme!

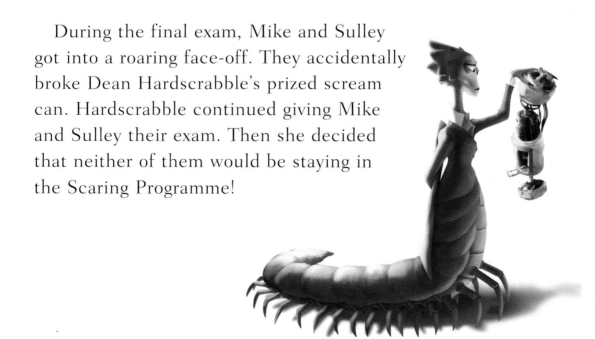

Winning the annual Scare Games was Mike and Sulley's only way of getting back into the Scaring Programme. To compete in the games, they had to join a fraternity. They joined the least scary group on campus: Oozma Kappa. The members of OK were Don, Squishy, Art and Terri and Terry.

Mike wasn't happy about working with Sulley – but he had no choice.

The first Scare Games event was the Toxicity Challenge. The teams had to get from one end of a sewer tunnel to the other while avoiding stinging glow urchins. The second the race started, Mike and Sulley took off and left the rest of the OKs behind. The entire team ended up coming in last. Oozma Kappa was out!

Then, suddenly, one of the winning teams was disqualified for cheating. The OKs were back in!

The next day, the OKs showed Mike some of their talents, but Mike already had a plan. "From now on we are of one mind ... *my* mind," he said.

Sulley rolled his eyes. "You tell them what to do, but not me. Later coach," he muttered.

The second event, Avoid the Parent, took place in the library. The teams had to capture their flag without getting caught by the librarian! Even though Sulley was no help to the team at all, the OKs managed to take fourth place. Squishy had grabbed the flag and made it out of the library without anyone noticing!

Just as the OKs were starting to feel confident, the RORs made fun of them. They told the OKs they'd never be real Scarers.

Mike decided to take everyone to Monsters, Inc. They sneaked up onto the roof and looked down onto a scare floor. They saw that Scarers came in all shapes and sizes. Everyone was inspired.

Mike and Sulley both admitted that they had been behaving badly. They agreed they needed to start working together.

The following morning, Mike and Sulley bounded
out of bed. They couldn't wait to begin training for
the next Scare Games event! They packed up their
gear, met up with the other OKs and headed off
to campus.

Mike worked on getting the team in tip-top shape.
He taught them how to sneak into a bedroom,
how to drop to the floor and how to dodge
teenagers. In between drills, Mike got
them to run on the spot and practise
their 'scary feet'.

The Oozma Kappas' training paid off. They passed
the Don't Scare the Teen event and moved to the next
round! Mike helped them to practise for the Hide and
Sneak event. The OKs were so well prepared, they came
in second.

They were heading to the finals!

Later, Sulley ran into Dean Hardscrabble.

"Tomorrow each of you must prove that you are undeniably scary, and I know one of you is not," she said.

Sulley knew that she meant Mike. He didn't want to believe her, but he couldn't help but wonder if she was right.

The RORs and the OKs were going head-to-head in
the final Scare Games event. Each competitor had to
perform a scare in a simulator.

Mike was the last member of the OKs to perform
his scare. He entered the room, sneaked up to the bed,
leapt up and roared! The robot child sat bolt upright
and screamed.

Mike's scare had given the OKs the highest score. They had won the Scare Games! Don, Squishy, Art, Terri and Terry and Sulley all surrounded Mike and lifted him on their shoulders. The entire amphitheatre burst into cheers and applause.

"We're in the Scaring Programme!" Sulley cried.

But the moment didn't last long. Mike soon discovered that Sulley had rigged the controls on the simulator. Mike's difficulty level had been switched to "easy". He couldn't believe it!

"Well, what was I supposed to do?" Sulley blurted out. "Let the whole team fail because you don't have it?"

Mike was angry. He stormed off and stole a key to the Door Tech Lab, where students learned how to build doors to the human world. He put a scream can in place, powered up a door – and opened it! Alarms went off all over campus, sending Hardscrabble and her security guards racing to the lab.

Mike found himself in the wardrobe of a child's room. He crept out towards the sleeping child and ... ROARED!

The youngster sat up and smiled. "You look funny," she said.

Mike couldn't believe it. Suddenly, he realized he wasn't in a child's bedroom. He turned to look and saw that he was in a cabin full of kids!

Meanwhile, Sulley rushed to the lab. He slipped past
security, ran through the door and went off to rescue Mike.
He found him beside a lake in the camp grounds.

"I thought I could show everybody that Mike Wazowski
is something special. But I'm just not," said Mike.

Sulley told Mike he wasn't much different. He had
messed things up his entire life. "I'll never know how you
feel, but you're not the only 'failure' here," he said.

Mike and Sulley returned to the cabin,
but the door back to Monsters University
had been powered down. They were
trapped! A group of adults were now
quickly approaching.

"If we really scare them, we could
generate enough scream to power the door
from this side," said Mike.

As the adults entered the cabin,
Mike and Sulley set up their big scare.
Then, on Mike's cue, Sulley loomed
over the adults and ROARED!

The adults screamed and ran for their lives. Back in the Door Tech Lab, the door's scream can filled to the brim! Hardscrabble watched in disbelief as the door exploded and Mike and Sulley blasted into the room.

They had performed an epic scare – but they still got expelled for breaking university rules. Mike and Sulley wondered about their plans for the future. Then Mike had an idea. "There's still one way we could work at a scare floor," he said.

They both got jobs in the Monsters, Inc. mailroom! Mike knew that if they worked hard enough, anything was possible.

This was just the beginning for Team Wazowski and Sullivan.